DISNEY'S THE LION KING

Based on the film of the same name from Walt Disney Pictures.

Canadian Cataloguing in Publication Data
Main entry under title:
The lion king
At head of title: Disney's.
ISBN 0-590-24336-5
I. Walt Disney Company.

PZ10.3.Li   1994   j813'.54   C94-931844-2

6 5 4 3 2 1   Printed in Canada   4 5 6 7 8/9

Scholastic Canada Ltd.

The African sun, huge and orange, rose over the horizon. Birds and animals stirred, and began to cross the plains to Pride Rock.

Silently they waited below the mountain of stone.

Rafiki, an old baboon, made his way through the crowd to greet Mufasa, the Lion King. Mufasa led Rafiki to a quiet spot where Sarabi, his queen, nestled with Simba, their newborn cub.

Rafiki leaned over the little cub and made a special mark on his forehead. Carefully he picked up Simba and carried him to the

very edge of Pride Rock. As he raised the little prince high above his head, a loud cheer of welcome rose from the animals below.

Giraffes, monkeys, zebras and elephants all bowed down before their future king.

Scar, the king's jealous brother, did not cheer. Simba's birth had removed his last hope of becoming king. "I was first in line," he growled, "until that little *hair ball* was born!"

Young Simba grew and learned. Mufasa showed his son the Pride Lands he would rule. "One day, Simba, the sun will set on my time here and will rise with you as the new king."

Mufasa warned Simba to stay away from the shadowy land in the distance.

4

"That's beyond our borders," he said. "You must never go there, Simba."

"But I thought a king can do whatever he wants," said Simba.

"There's more to being king than getting your way all the time," Mufasa told him.

Simba could hardly wait to become a king like his dad. "Hey, Uncle Scar!" he called. "Guess what? I'm gonna be king of Pride Rock! My dad just showed me the whole kingdom! And I'm gonna rule it all!"

"Oh, *goody*," sneered Scar. "Forgive me for *not* leaping for joy. Bad back, you know."

Simba did not know that his uncle hated him. Scar wanted to be king himself. He thought of a way to get rid of his young nephew.

"Your father showed you the whole kingdom, did he?" he asked innocently. "He didn't show you what's beyond that rise at the northern border?"

"Well, no," Simba said reluctantly. "He said I can't go there."

"He's absolutely right," Scar replied. "It's *far* too dangerous.

Only the *bravest* of lions go there."

"Well, I'm brave," said Simba. "What's out there?"

Scar told Simba that the shadowy land was really an elephant graveyard. He knew this would be too much for the young cub to resist.

Simba found his best friend, a young lioness named Nala, and asked her to go with him to a "really cool" place. It was not long before they arrived at the elephant graveyard, a frightening area full of bones and skulls.

"This is it! We made it!" Simba exclaimed.

Nala was impressed. "It's really creepy," she said.

Zazu, the king's trusted advisor, tracked the cubs down before they had a chance to explore. The worried hornbill had come to take them home. "Right now we are all in very real danger," he scolded.

"Danger?" asked Simba. "Ha! I walk on the wild side. I laugh in the face of danger. Ha-ha-ha-ha-ha!"

An eerie laugh echoed from one of the elephant skulls as three ugly hyenas slipped out from the darkness. The hyenas were hungry. They wanted nice, juicy lion cubs for dinner!

Soon Simba and Nala were being chased across the graveyard. When they tried to climb over a large elephant skeleton, the dry bones snapped. They were trapped inside.

Simba was terrified. He tried to roar like a lion, but all that came out was a little squeak. It looked as if he and Nala would become the hyenas' dinner after all.

Suddenly Mufasa appeared. With a furious roar, he attacked the hyenas and sent them flying.

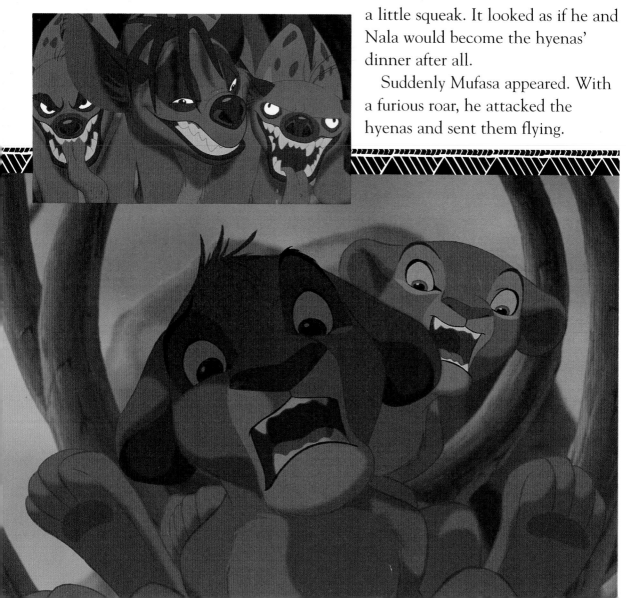

Then Simba had to face his father's anger. "Simba, I'm very disappointed in you," Mufasa growled. "You could have been killed! You deliberately disobeyed me. And what's worse, you put Nala in danger!"

"I was just trying to be brave, like you," Simba said, and started to cry. "You're not scared of anything."

"I was today," Mufasa said. "I thought I might lose you." He pulled his young son close. A few moments later they were laughing, romping and playing together.

"Dad?" asked Simba. "We're pals, right? And we'll always be together, right?"

Mufasa gazed up at the night sky. "Look at the stars," he told his son. "The great kings of the past look down on us from those stars. Remember that those kings will always be there to guide you . . . and so will I."

Back at the hyenas' lair, Scar was furious. His plot to get rid of Simba had failed. "I practically gift-wrapped those cubs for you," he snarled, "and you couldn't even dispose of them."

Scar told the hyenas about a new plan to eliminate both Simba and Mufasa. "Then I will be king!" he shouted. "Stick with me and you'll never go hungry again!"

The very next day Scar took Simba into the gorge. "Your father has a *marvellous* surprise for you," he lied. "Just stay on this rock."

While Simba waited, Scar climbed to the top of the ridge overlooking the gorge. When Scar gave the signal, the hyenas started to chase a herd of frightened wildebeest into the gorge—and straight toward Simba.

Startled by the sound of hooves, Simba began to run for his life.

The wildebeest were faster. Desperately, the cub raced up the branch of
a dead tree. As the herd of animals stormed past, the tree started to shake.

Scar told Mufasa what was happening. "Quick! Stampede! In the gorge! Simba's down there!" he called.

Mufasa raced into the gorge to save his only son. He arrived just as the tree branch broke, and snatched Simba out of the path of the stampede. As he placed the cub on a safe ledge, a galloping wildebeest knocked Mufasa back into the herd.

With a mighty effort, the wounded king scrambled up the loose rock at the side of the gorge. Bruised and weak, he kept slipping back. As he

looked up, Mufasa saw his wicked brother waiting at the top of the cliff. "Scar, help me!" he called.

Scar reached down to Mufasa and pulled him close. "Long live the king," he whispered, and let go of his brother's arms. Mufasa fell back into the gorge and disappeared under the thundering hooves.

Although he could not see Scar, Simba saw his father fall. "Nooooo!" he screamed as he raced into the dust-filled gorge. He found Mufasa lying on the ground.

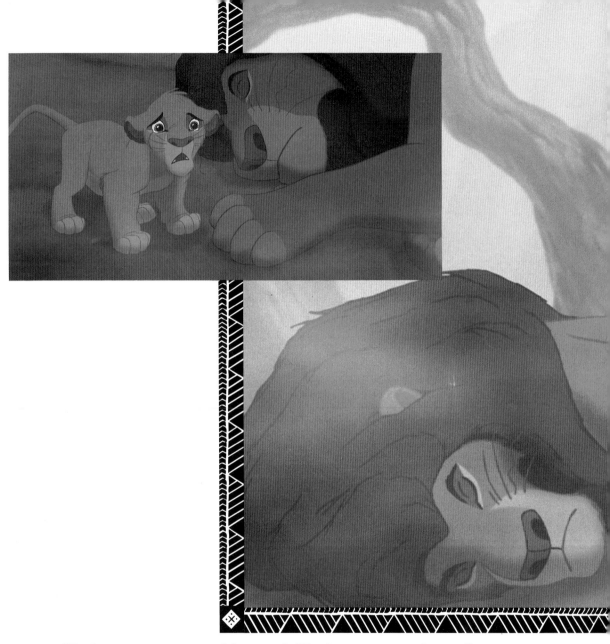

"Dad, you gotta get up," he cried. "Dad, we gotta go home."

Slowly Simba realized his father was dead. They would never talk or play together again. His father would never hold him again. It was more than the young cub could bear, and he sobbed into the great lion's mane.

Scar arrived a few moments later. "Simba, what have you *done?*" he asked in an accusing tone of voice.

Simba tried to explain. "There were wildebeests . . . and he tried to save me . . . it was an accident! I didn't mean for it to . . ."

Scar saw his opportunity. "Of course, of course you didn't," he said. "No one *ever* means for these things to happen. But the king is dead. If it weren't for *you*, he'd still be alive."

"What am I gonna do?" asked Simba.

"Run away, Simba!" said Scar. "Run away and never return!"

Simba set off as fast as he could go. When the hyenas appeared, Scar ordered them to hunt down Simba. He wanted to make sure that his nephew would never come back.

The hyenas chased after Simba. He leaped over a ledge and landed

painfully in the middle of a thorn patch. The hyenas did not want to fight
their way through the thorns to reach Simba, so they let him go. "If you
ever come back, we'll kill you!" they yelled. Their voices echoed across
the plains as the young prince fled.

Safe from the hyenas, Simba trudged on across grassland, wasteland, and desert. There was no place for him to go. After battling his way through a sandstorm, Simba collapsed, tired and thirsty. The vultures began to circle.

Fortunately, a warthog and a meerkat arrived just in time to carry the cub to the safety and shade of the jungle. A few minutes later, Simba opened his eyes.

"I saved you," announced Timon, the small meerkat. At a snort from the warthog, he added, "Well, Pumbaa helped. A little. So, where ya from?"

"Who cares?" said Simba. "I can't go back."

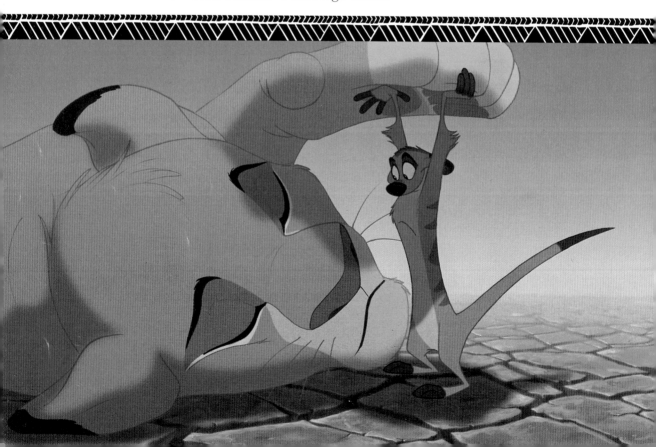

"Ah, you're an outcast," exclaimed Timon. "That's great! So are we!"

Simba did not tell them what had happened. It was too terrible. Timon and Pumbaa didn't seem to mind, though. "Put your past behind you," said Timon. "Repeat after me: *Hakuna Matata.* It means no worries."

Before long, Simba was living in a jungle paradise with his new friends. They taught him to eat bugs for dinner. They played all day, and they gazed at the stars at night. Simba learned to say "*Hakuna Matata,*" but sometimes it just didn't feel right.

Time passed and Simba grew into a young lion. One day, when Pumbaa and Timon were hunting bugs, a lioness attacked Pumbaa. Simba jumped in the fight to save his friend. The lioness fought well, though, and she quickly pinned Simba to the ground. Simba thought he recognized her.

"Nala? Is that really you?" he asked.

Nala backed away in shock. "Who are you?"

When she realized that it was her old friend Simba, Nala exclaimed, "Oh, it's great to see you! Wait till everyone finds out you've been here all this time!"

"Nobody has to know," Simba said quickly.

"Of course they do!" Nala insisted. "Everyone thinks you're dead. You're alive! And that means . . . you're the king!"

"No, I'm not the king," Simba replied sadly. "Maybe I was gonna be, but that was a long time ago."

Tears came to Nala's eyes as she explained what had happened since Simba had left home. Scar had allowed the hyenas to take over the Pride Lands. Everything had been destroyed. There was no food or water. Nala begged Simba to come back with her before everyone starved.

Simba knew he could not go back. If it wasn't for him, his father would still be alive. "*Hakuna Matata*," was all he would say, and he walked off to be by himself.

A funny little baboon started to follow Simba through the jungle. "*Asante sana. Squash banana*," he sang.

Finally Simba snapped, "Would you stop following me? Who are you?"

It was Rafiki, the wise one. He told Simba that Mufasa was still alive, and offered to take the young lion to meet his father. He led Simba to a shimmering pool of water. "Look down there," Rafiki said.

"That's not my father. It's just my reflection," Simba said, disappointed.

"No . . . look *harder*," Rafiki insisted.

Simba gazed back into the water and saw his father's face suddenly appear inside his own.

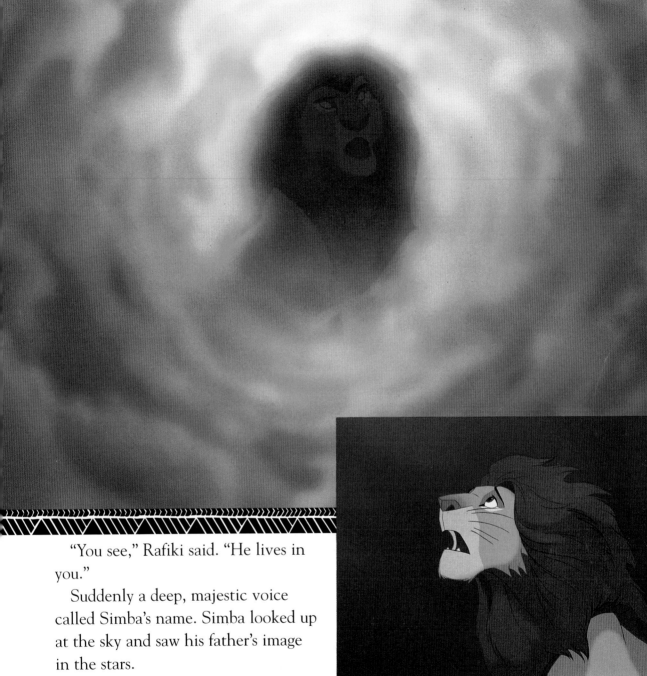

"You see," Rafiki said. "He lives in you."

Suddenly a deep, majestic voice called Simba's name. Simba looked up at the sky and saw his father's image in the stars.

"Simba, you must take your place in the Circle of Life," the voice said. "You are my son and the one true king." As the vision faded, Simba knew he had to stop running away from the past. It was time to go home.

When he arrived back at the Pride Lands, Simba was horrified. Everywhere he looked he saw destruction. "I didn't want to believe you," he said to Nala when she joined him, "but now I'm ready to try to do something about this."

"We'll do it together," Nala said.

At that moment, Timon and Pumbaa caught up with the lions. "At your service, my liege!" Pumbaa said as he bowed before Simba.

The young lion led his army of four toward Pride Rock. They peered from behind a large boulder at the fierce, hungry hyenas that were guarding the kingdom. Simba gave them all instructions. "Nala, you find my mother and rally the lionesses. I'll look for Scar. Timon and Pumbaa, you create a diversion."

As Pumbaa and Timon began to dance in front of the guards, Nala and Simba slipped away.

At Pride Rock, hungry hyenas were complaining to Scar that the lionesses would not hunt for them any more. Sarabi, who led the lionesses, told Scar that all the herds had left. There was nothing for them to hunt.

"If you were half the king Mufasa was . . . " Sarabi began.

Scar cut her off. "I am ten times the king *Mufasa* was," he bellowed, and he struck the queen with his paw. Mufasa's name echoed off the cliffs.

High on a rock above, Simba saw his uncle strike his mother. He charged down to attack. For a moment, Scar backed up in fear, thinking he was face to face with Mufasa. Then he realized it was only Simba. Scar grew bolder. He had always been able to control the young lion.

Simba told Scar that he was no longer king. "Step down, Scar," he ordered.

"You see them," Scar answered calmly, pointing to the army of hyenas. "*They* think I'm king."

"Step down or fight," insisted Simba.

Sweetly, Scar continued talking. "Must this all end in violence? I'd hate to be responsible for the death of a family member." He knew where Simba's weak spot was. "Wouldn't you agree, Simba?"

"That's not going to work, Scar," replied Simba.

Scar backed Simba toward the edge of the cliff, challenging his nephew to tell everyone who was responsible for Mufasa's death. Simba knew he had to admit it. "I am," he said. All the lionesses gasped.

Scar continued to press forward. "Simba, you're in trouble now. But this time daddy isn't here to save you. And now everyone knows *why*."

Simba lost his footing and slipped over the edge of the cliff. As he grasped at the edge, Scar peered over at him. "This is just the way your father looked before he died," smiled Scar, relishing the moment. "And here's my little secret . . . *I killed Mufasa*."

Furious, Simba leaped back on the cliff to confront Scar. "Murderer!" he roared. The hills rang with the accusation.

Scar called out for the hyenas. The lionesses dove into the battle. Claws slashed and hyenas flew. Zazu joined in the fight, and Timon and Pumbaa charged in. Lightning forked and thunder boomed. In the confusion, Scar tried to slip away.

In a flash, Simba was after him, racing through the fire caused by the lightning. Soon the two enemies stood face to face at the top of Pride Rock. Scar was cornered.

"Simba," he begged. "Have mercy. The hyenas are to blame. *They* are the enemy. It was their fault." He did not know that the hyenas were nearby, listening. Although they had come to help Scar, the hyenas turned and left when they heard what he said.

Scar started to tremble. "Are you going to kill me?" he asked.

"No, I'm not like you," Simba replied. "Run away, Scar, and never return."

Scar pretended to slink away, then suddenly turned and lunged.
Simba was ready, and he knocked Scar over the edge of the rock with a
swipe of his mighty paw.

Down below, Scar saw the hyenas coming towards him. "My friends,"
he smiled.

"Your *enemy*," one of them said menacingly. "Remember?"

Soon the whole pack of hyenas was circling around Scar. They
laughed eerily as they moved in closer, eyes gleaming. Scar was never
seen again.

Simba limped down from the mountain and gave a great roar of victory.
The lionesses responded with joy as it began to rain. Life had been
restored to the Pride Lands.

Some time later, a brilliant African sun dawned over the plain. Birds and animals made their way to Pride Rock, where they waited as Rafiki blessed a tiny lion cub.

When Rafiki carried the cub to the edge of the rock and raised him high above his head, a roar of welcome arose from the animals.

Giraffes, monkeys, zebras and elephants all bowed down to the new prince, the son of Simba and Nala. And the Circle of Life continued . . .